To:. Mrs. Rutl...

Love,Sam Stewart

To:. Mrs. Rutl...

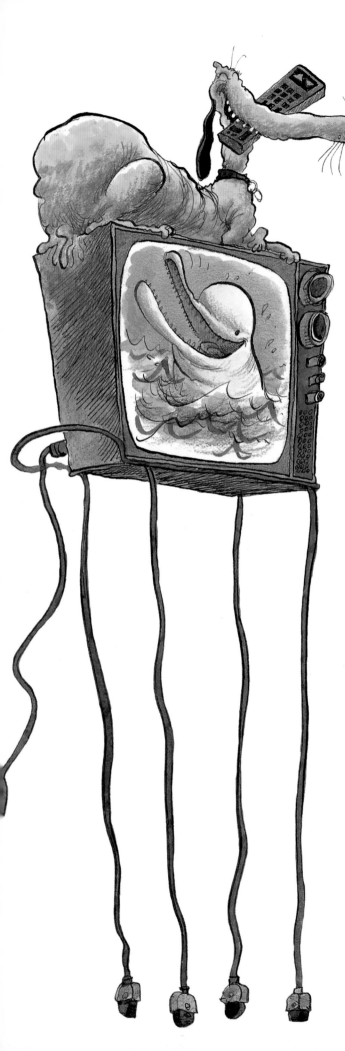

To Simone and Andrew,
two great kids who always sing
silly dilly songs of love
—A. K

To Bubbies,
a silly, silly citizen
—D. C.

Margaret K. McElderry Books
An imprint of Simon & Schuster Children's Publishing Division
1230 Avenue of the Americas
New York, NY 10020

Book design by Sonia Chaghatzbanian
The text of the this book is set in Kosmik.
The illustrations are rendered in watercolors, colored pencil, and ink.

Printed in the United States of America

30 29 28 27 26 25 24 23 22 21 20

Library of Congress Cataloging-in-Publication Data:
Katz, Alan.
Take me out of the bathtub and other silly dilly songs / Alan Katz ; illustrated by
David Catrow.-1st ed.
p. cm.
Summary: Well-known songs, including "Oh, Susannah" and "Row, Row, Row Your
Boat," are presented with new words and titles, such as "I'm So Carsick" and "Go Go
Go to Bed."

ISBN 0-689-82903-5

1. Children's songs—United States—Texts. 2. Humorous songs—Texts. [1. Humorous
songs. 2. Songs.] I. Catrow, David, ill. II. Title.
PZ8.3.K1275 Tak 2001
782.42164'0268-dc21
[E]
99-089390

take me out of the bathtub

and other silly dilly songs

by Alan Katz

illustrated by David Catrow

Margaret K. McElderry Books
New York London Toronto Sydney Singapore

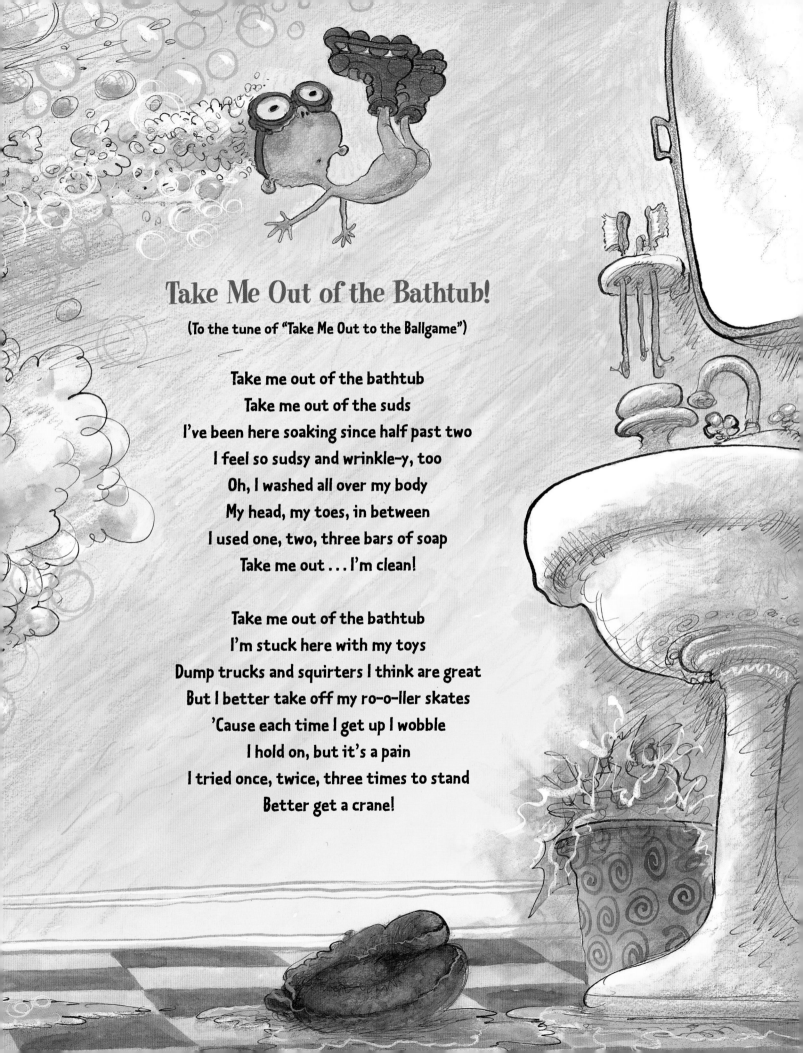

Take Me Out of the Bathtub!

(To the tune of "Take Me Out to the Ballgame")

Take me out of the bathtub
Take me out of the suds
I've been here soaking since half past two
I feel so sudsy and wrinkle-y, too
Oh, I washed all over my body
My head, my toes, in between
I used one, two, three bars of soap
Take me out . . . I'm clean!

Take me out of the bathtub
I'm stuck here with my toys
Dump trucks and squirters I think are great
But I better take off my ro-o-ller skates
'Cause each time I get up I wobble
I hold on, but it's a pain
I tried once, twice, three times to stand
Better get a crane!

The Yogurt Flies Straight
From My Brother

(To the tune of "My Bonnie Lies Over the Ocean")

The yogurt flies straight from my brother
The peaches zoom toward me from sis
When she gets home I bet my mother
Says we shouldn't food fight like this!

Food fight! Food fight!
There's food on the counter and chairs! And chairs!
Food fight! Food fight!
There's tons of meat loaf in my hair!

My brother flicks peas with his fork and
They zip down my shirt with a splat
Next I see a big piece of pork land
On my head like it's a new hat!

Food fight! Food fight!
Clean up, there is no time to spare, to spare
Food fight! Food fight!
Got carrots in my underwear!

We should stop, but it's so much fun that
I yell for one more ice-cream bomb
It soars down the hall to the front door
And into the face of . . . our mom!

Food fight! Food fight!
There'll be no more food fights for me, for me
Food fight! Food fight!
I'm grounded till I'm twenty-three!

I've Been Cleaning Up My Bedroom

(To the tune of "I've Been Working on the Railroad")

I've been cleaning up my bedroom, all the livelong day
I've been cleaning up my bedroom, just to put my stuff away
Mom says, "Tidy up that pile
Sitting on the floor."
I just nod to her, then smile
And shove it out the door!

Please clean up this mess
Please clean up this mess
Please clean up this mess today-ay-ay
Please clean up this mess
Please clean up this mess
That is all my mom can say.

Someone put my mitt in the corner
Someone threw my pants in a heap-eap-eap-eap
Someone put my games on the bed, and
So on the floor I'll sleep.
It's messy.

Three flies nibble over there
Must be the sandwich on the chair-air-air-air
Three flies nibble over there
Come help me clean if you dare!

Stinky Stinky Diaper Change

(To the tune of "Twinkle, Twinkle, Little Star")

Stinky stinky diaper change
Boy, my brother smells so strange
He made something in his pants
Sure hope it won't attract ants
Stinky stinky diaper change
Boy, my brother smells so strange!

It's okay, don't hold your nose
Now he's clean and in fresh clothes
All his stuff is often stained
Can't wait till he's potty trained
He's so cute in his playpen
What's that smell? Oh . . . not again!

Brother Mitch

(To the tune of "London Bridge")

Brother Mitch keeps falling down
Throughout town
He's a clown
When he falls he wears a frown
Tie his laces!

Double knots will tie them tight
He falls left
He falls right
He's a walking bandage sight
Tie his laces!

Tie them twenty times and then
Not again!
They're open!
Think I got a better plan
Buy him Velcro!

Go Go Go to Bed

(To the tune of "Row, Row, Row Your Boat")

Go go go to bed
Put your head at rest
Or tomorrow while at school
You'll snooze on your desk!

No no no not yet
There's more stuff to do
Art and games and balls and cards
Plus some TV, too!

Whoa whoa whoa slow down
Not another peep
You are young and I am old
We both need some sleep!

Oh oh oh wait, Mom
Just ten minutes, please
Yawn, I wanna play some more
Yawn, um, good night . . . zzzzzzz!

Bobby, Put the TV On

(To the tune of "Polly, Put the Kettle On")

Bobby put the TV on
Bobby put the TV on
Bobby put the TV on
To Channel 3.

Suzie changed to 28
Suzie said, "This show looks great"
Bobby yelled, "Hey sister, wait!"
And changed it back.

28 . . . and then it's 3
They were flipping wildly
What a battle, poor TV
They can't agree!

Bobby said, "Okay, let's vote"
Suzie then grabbed the remote
They were at each other's throats
When in came Dad.

Dad said, "I'm ashamed of you"
And I know just what to do
Let's watch sports on 22 . . .

The kids rode bikes!

Cranky Poodle

(To the tune of "Yankee Doodle")

Cranky Poodle in my home
Clawing, scratching, howling
Scaring people, scaring cats
Unrolling paper toweling.

Cranky Poodle drives me nuts
Most days I can't bear it
Wish my folks would trade her for
A hamster or a parrot!

I took Cranky for a walk
Although I hate to mention
She pulled me halfway down the block
To chase a fire engine.

Cranky Poodle, you're a pest
Wish you were a guppy
Oh no! Guess what mom told me
Our poodle just had puppies!

Ripped My Favorite T-Shirt

(To the tune of "I'm a Little Teapot")

Ripped my favorite T-shirt
Scuffed my shoes
Lost my red sweater
And more bad news . . .

Bet my mom gets steamed up
She will grouse
'Cause I haven't left the house!

Broke my grandma's teacup
Scraped her floor
Smeared paint on her kitchen door
Now she will get angry
There's no doubt
Oops, I just locked Grandma out!

I'm a little angel
Every day
But trouble finds me
Come what may
Played the drums and just popped
Mom's soufflé
When I sleep she yells . . . hooray!

Sock in the Gravy

(To the tune of "Rockabye Baby")

Sock in the gravy
Glove in the soup
Tie in the meat loaf
And here's a scoop . . .
If you don't like clothes in your baked beans
Don't cook your food in washing machines!

To write a report
On dairy food
Go hit the books
And remember, too . . .
You will get good grades (and you'll stay alive)
By not putting cheese in dad's disk drive!

Give Me a Break

(To the tune of "Home on the Range")

Oh give me a break
'Cause I made a mistake
And my library book's overdue
The fault is all mine
Oh boy, what a fine
It was due way back in '92!

Home, home's where it's hid
This is such a bad thing that I did
And you might say, "Gee whiz!"
'Cause the book's title is
How to Be a Responsible Kid!

I Have a Baby-sitter Here with Me

(To the tune of "I Have a Little Baby Bumblebee")

I have a baby-sitter here with me
She's on the phone while she's watching TV
I thought she was supposed to play with me
Now ... she's hungry!

My baby-sitter's gonna raid the snacks
Cookies, candy, a box of Cracker Jack
She chomped so fast that right before my eyes
She ... ate the prize!

Wait till my parents come home, what a fit
Bet they'll never ask her back to si-it
Oh no, what am I saying? I'd miss her
She's ... my sister!

I'm Filthy, I'm Dirty

(To the tune of "It's Raining, It's Pouring")

I'm filthy, I'm dirty
Got mud on my shirt-y
On a whim
I took a swim
In a puddle with a birdie!

I'm smelly, I'm dusty
From head to toe I'm musty
To be a slob's
A full-time job
I guess I look digust-y.

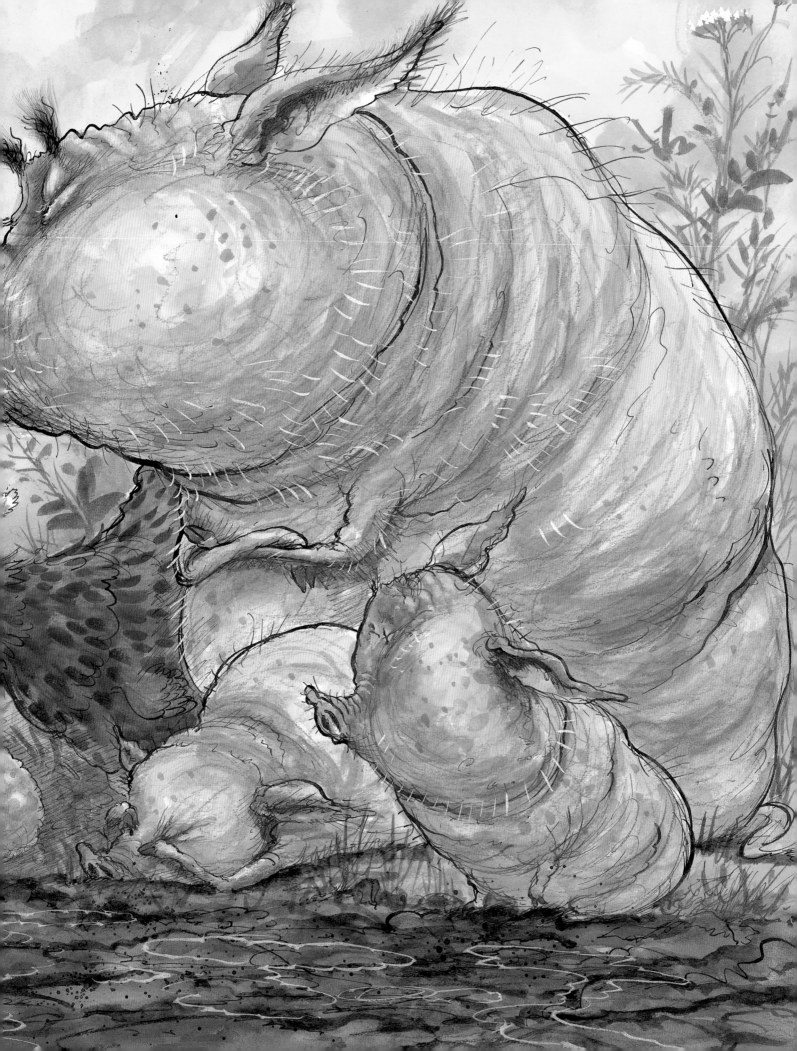

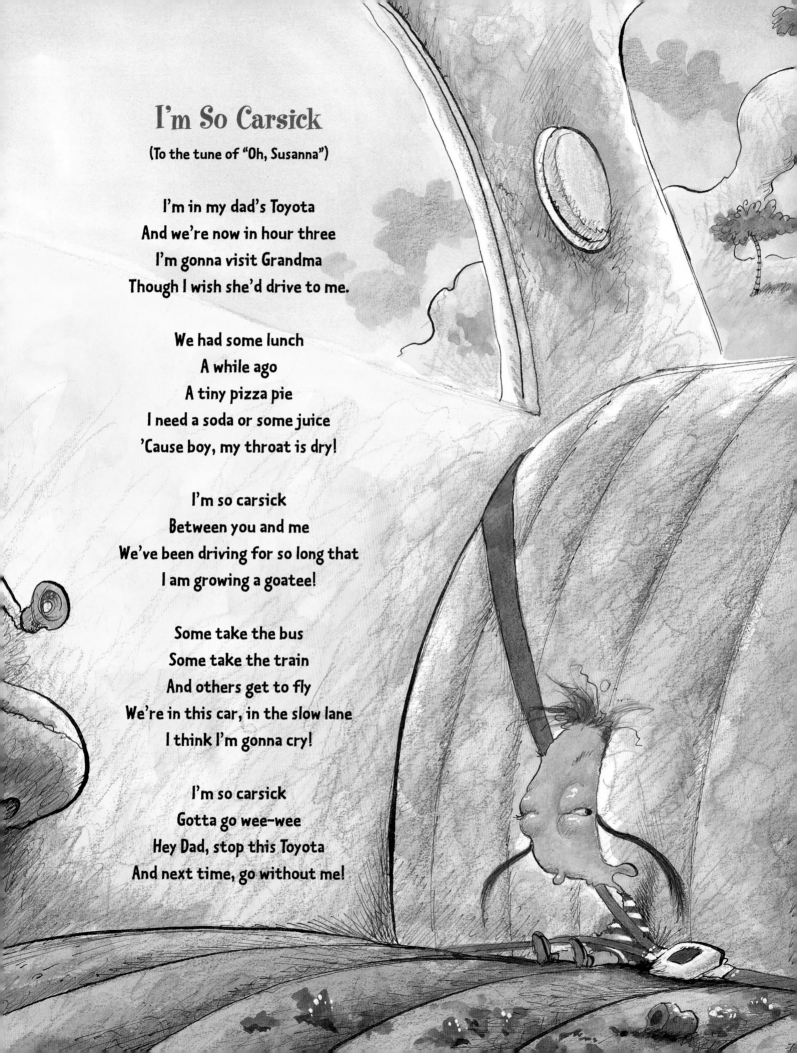

I'm So Carsick

(To the tune of "Oh, Susanna")

I'm in my dad's Toyota
And we're now in hour three
I'm gonna visit Grandma
Though I wish she'd drive to me.

We had some lunch
A while ago
A tiny pizza pie
I need a soda or some juice
'Cause boy, my throat is dry!

I'm so carsick
Between you and me
We've been driving for so long that
I am growing a goatee!

Some take the bus
Some take the train
And others get to fly
We're in this car, in the slow lane
I think I'm gonna cry!

I'm so carsick
Gotta go wee-wee
Hey Dad, stop this Toyota
And next time, go without me!